Ivor the Invisible

First published in 2001 by Channel 4 Books, an imprint of Pan Macmillan Ltd,
20 New Wharf Road, London N1 9RR, Basingstoke and Oxford.

Associated companies throughout the world.

www.panmacmillan.com

ISBN 0 7522 2034 9

Pictures and text © 2001 Screen First Limited

9 8 7 6 5 4 3 2 1

A CIP catalogue record for this book is available from the British Library.

Design by Dan Newman/Perfect Bound
Printed by Bath Press

This book accompanies the animated film *Ivor the Invisible*,
produced by Screen First Ltd for Channel 4.
Director and storyboard: Hilary Audus
Producer: Paul Madden
Art Director: Sue Tong

IVOR
THE INVISIBLE

Story by

RAYMOND BRIGGS

WHUMP

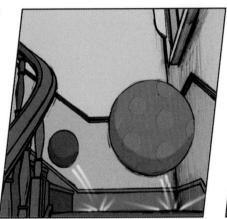
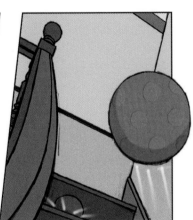

Ooh! Get off!

Hey!

Be...My...Friend

Who are you?
Where are you?

Ha haa!

Where are you?
Are you still here?

THUD!

Is that you?
How big are you?

There's miles
of you!

You're bigger
than an
elephant!

Where's your
face?

Do you have a face?
I hope so.

OK. You win.
You don't want to
be measured.
I suppose it is a bit
rude to measure
someone you've
only just met...

9

Tell me your name, please — write it.

I – V – o?

Ivor, you mean?

Oh, NO!

You mean no? Oh, OK... Well I'll just have to call you Ivor then!

Hello Ivor – I'm John.

Mike, Mike!
Help!

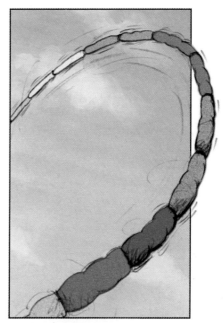

Freak wind –
a whirlwind...

?

HISSSSS

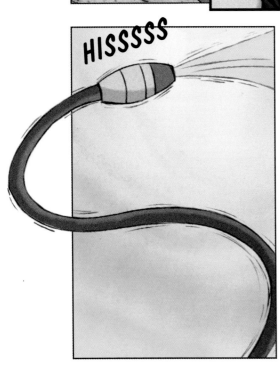

LATER...

Teatime!

OK, coming!

THUMP!

What on earth are you doing?

I bumped into something. A force field. An invisible force field.

Squish

14

TEATIME

clink!

squish!

SPLASH!

clang!

tink

I'm going home.

I'm sorry Barbs...
I don't know what's
happening.

I'll get your
coat

If this goes on we'll have to move.

Haunted.
A haunted house.

We'll never sell it.
A haunted house.

The washing-up was handy, though...

Ivor, do you sleep?
Even fish sleep,
so they say.

Do invisible giants sleep?
It seems they eat. So do
they do invisible poos?

Are there great heaps of
invisible poo all over the
place and we don't know?

Oh, I see – you want to be like me, you mean?

Bit difficult to be normal, if you're invisible...

...and keep changing shape.

Well, you'd better come up the park with me tomorrow...

That's normal.

How do you do that?

Magic! It's all me!

THWACK!

Ooh!

Gasp!

Ivor!

You idiot!

Squeal!

Eek!

Yes, I think I'll get down now!

Hey, Mister. Can I be in your gang?

Er... OK

I really like...

...ducks.

SQUAWK!

THUMP!

Oof
Huff
Puff

Hey! Wha—

23

SPLAT!

Ha Ha Haaa!

RUMBLE
RUMBLE

What's all this, John? What's going on?

It's my friend Ivor. He's huge. He's invisible. He says I musn't tell you about him.

You shouldn't have told me, it was a secret.

He's getting to be a real pain.

THE NEXT MORNING...

Wan go School be lik you

Go... to... school?

Well... I don't know...

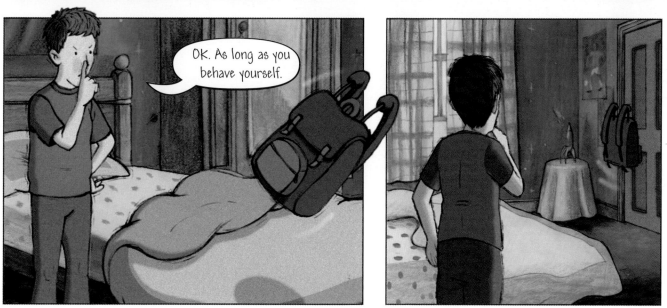

OK. As long as you behave yourself.

AT SCHOOL...

Pay attention, everybody...

Ha ha haa!

Oh no! Ivor's in here!

Alright. You can go.

Oh no! No! You **idiot!**

You're **such** a loony!

You're not invisible carrying those!

They'll have followed you!

There's a whole crowd of people...

36

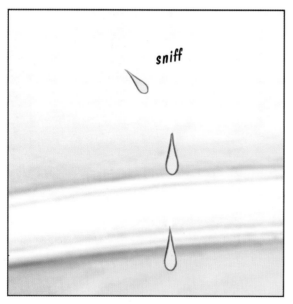

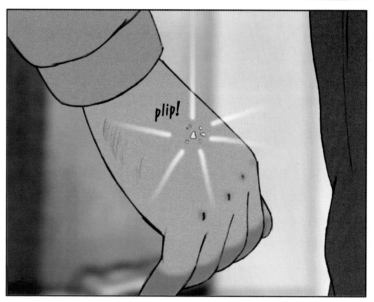

I'll have to tell them my invisible friend...

...has disappeared.

BONK
BONK

Bye bye!